JAKE

ALL THE SINGLE DADS BOOK TWO

SADIE KING

ALL THE SINGLE DADS

These single dad hotties are fiercely protective and will do anything for the ones they love.

The series features grumpy single dads, secret billionaires, shy neighbors, and men turned obsessive by the curvy heroines who capture their hearts.

Each book in the series is a standalone but best enjoyed together. And look out for your favorite characters from Maple Springs popping in for cameo appearances.

All the Single Dads

Jaxon – Kali & Jaxon

Jake – Fiona & Jake

Levi – Aria & Levi

Brock – Olive & Brock

Anton – Eden & Anton

Xavier – Angela & Xavier

Maple Springs

Small Town Sisters

Candy's Café

All the Single Dads

Men of Maple Mountain

JAKE

ALL THE SINGLE DADS BOOK TWO

The perfect fling just got complicated...

Jake

I haven't done relationships ever since my ex ran off and left me as a single parent.

There's only one thing I need from a woman, and when I meet the curvy Fiona, I know she'll satisfy my needs.

Only she gets under my skin. She makes me laugh and makes me remember what it feels like to love.

But before I can tell her how I feel, she's gone.

I don't have her number; I don't even know her last name. Now I must hunt her down and claim her as my own.

Fiona

I came to the spa resort to relax, and if that means flirting with the hot guy who slides into the Jacuzzi next to me, then I will.

He tells me in no uncertain terms that this is a casual thing, and I'm down with that. Until I'm not.

When I have to leave unexpectedly, I never think I'll see Jake again.

But life is full of uncertainty and surprises. And Jake's about to get the surprise of his life.

Jake is a single dad, secret baby instalove romance featuring an obsessed OTT hero and the curvy girl he claims as his own. No cliffhangers and with a happily ever after guaranteed.

JAKE

"Be good for your Uncle Nick."

"Okay Daddy," comes the earnest reply down the line.

My phone's pressed to my ear as I dump my duffle bag on the floor of the lobby. There's a tremor in Riley's voice. It's the first time I've left her alone for the night, and she's being as brave as an almost three-year-old can be.

"I'll be home in two sleeps," I try to reassure her.

Her voice wobbles. "Who's going to put me to bed?"

She's breaking my heart, and I think about turning around and driving home, but this is the first weekend I've had on my own since her mother left.

My buddy, Anton, has booked us into a mountain resort for a weekend of fishing and hiking. I haven't done either of those things since I was left as the sole parent for Riley. I love my daughter, but I've been looking forward to this for weeks.

"Uncle Nick or Aunty Zoey will put you to bed, pumpkin."

"And Sheepy?"

She's referring to her favorite soft toy.

"Yup, they'll tuck Sheepy in as well."

"Okay Daddy."

With bedtime sorted, she seems happier.

"Love you, pumpkin."

"Love you too, Daddy."

My heart warms at the words.

"Can you put your uncle on please?"

I hear a clatter as she puts the phone down, and then my brother's voice comes down the line.

"What's up?"

"She sleeps with a toy called Sheepy. We have this whole routine where she pretends to brush Sheepy's teeth before she does her own. But you'll have to do hers for her. She can't do it herself yet."

"Sheepy, got it."

I scratch my beard, wondering what I've forgotten. "I packed two sets of pajamas, but it's quite warm so you'll want to put her in the summer set. But then use the thicker blanket. There are band-aids and baby Tylenol in the bag…"

"Jake…" My brother interrupts, "she'll be fine."

I swallow. It's the first time I've left my baby in someone else's care for more than a few hours.

"We've got this. You go and relax."

He's right. God knows I need a break. I just worry about my princess and how she'll cope without me.

"I've left the name and number of the hotel in case you can't get ahold of me, but I'll have my phone on me at all times. If anything happens, give me a call and I'll come straight back."

"Jake. Stop worrying." There's a warning note to his voice. "Go and enjoy yourself. You deserve it."

Something flashes in my memory. "She likes warm milk before bed, heated a little from a cup, not a bottle. Although I packed the bottle just in case."

"I'm hanging up now."

"About forty seconds in the microwave, but test it first. That thing can get hot."

"Bye Jake."

The phone goes dead, and I stare at it for a minute. My brother just hung up on me. As I'm staring at the blank screen, a message comes through.

"We'll be okay. Relax and enjoy yourself."

I sigh. He's right. I'm here to relax. Riley has spent loads of time around Nick and Zoey. She'll be fine.

I'm just going to do some fishing, have a few beers with my buddy. I might even try out the spa facilities.

I pick up my bag to head over to check-in and just then my phone rings. It's Anton.

"Hey man, I've just arrived. Are you here yet?"

'I'm so sorry to do this to you, but Marcus is sick."

My heart sinks. Anton is one of the other single dads in Maple Springs, and we'd planned this weekend trip months ago. I know what's coming.

"Is he okay?"

"He's got a fever and vomiting. Probably just a bug. You know what kids are like."

I do. They pick up everything and always at the most inconvenient times.

"Sorry to do this, man, but my little guy needs me."

When you're a dad, your kid always comes first. Always.

"It's fine, man. You gotta do what you gotta do."

"We've got a boat booked tomorrow if you still want it. I'll send you the details."

"Sounds good. Hope Marcus gets better soon."

"Thanks man. Sorry to leave you on your own. I hope you can still enjoy the break."

I hang up the phone and slip it into my pocket. I've just gone from having a buddies fishing weekend to flying solo at a mountain resort.

With a sigh, I pick up my bag and head to the reception desk.

There's a woman in front of me, and I dump my bag on the ground behind her. She's wearing shiny high heels, and my eyes trace the length of her legs up to her substantial ass.

I can see every curve highlighted by her butt-hugging skirt. She shifts the weight onto her other leg, and her hips dip. Her rump slides to the other side and all those curves with it.

She's leaning over the reception desk and her skirt rides up, revealing the pale skin of her thigh. My pants twitch as my eyes rove up her legs, wondering what she feels like under that tight skirt.

My eyes continue up her body, over that glorious ass and to the long dark hair that falls down her back. Thick hair I'd like to twist in my hand as I have her on all fours.

I've got instant wood, and I haven't even seen her face yet.

The receptionist hands the woman a room key. I note

it's just the one. She's travelling alone. She half turns around to get her suitcase, and fuck me, she's a beauty, with a sweet oval face and full plump lips.

Her breasts are as curvaceous as her ass and just as grabbable. She turns around fully, and our eyes meet.

They're deep green and electric. Her mouth pops open like she's surprised to see me. She probably caught me looking at her tits. But I don't care. A woman this good looking needs to be admired.

"Excuse me." Her voice is soft and lyrical.

I realize I've put my duffle bag down on her purse.

"Sorry."

I pick it up, and she pulls her bag out.

"You here for the fishing or the hiking?" I ask.

Dressed like she is I'm pretty sure it's neither, and I'm right. She rewards me with a smile.

"I'm here for the spa."

"Girls weekend away?"

It's a loaded question. I want to find out if she's here with a man, and she knows it.

She shakes her head. "Just me. Getting some alone time."

She's here on her own, which suits me fine. She might want some company later.

"I'm Jake."

I offer my hand, and she takes it. "Fiona."

Her hand feels small in mine and delicate. Her skin is soft and warm, and I imagine that's what her thighs would feel like if I could run my hands up them.

She looks like a nice girl, a sweet smile on her lips, but I don't care about nice. Since my ex ran off, there's only one thing I need from a woman. And the pressure in my jeans tells me it's been too long since I got it.

"Are you checking in, sir?"

The receptionist sounds irritated, and I guess it's because there's a line of people behind me.

Fiona takes the handle of her suitcase.

"Enjoy your weekend, Jake."

I watch her go, her ass swaying enticingly.

Everyone keeps telling me to relax and enjoy my weekend, and now I know exactly how I'm going to do just that.

2

FIONA

I feel the tension melting out of my shoulders, and I sink into the water a little deeper. With the bubbles against my back and the gentle gurgling of the water, I feel myself start to relax for the first time in months. I take a deep breath and close my eyes.

My mind wanders to Mom and if she's okay without me.

Since she got sick, I've been looking after her pretty much 24/7. Occasionally my brother flies in for the weekend to visit and give me a break. This time he insisted I get away for some proper time to myself. He booked me this spa weekend and instructed me to relax.

There's a splash next to me, and I open my eyes in time to see a slick body slide into the opposite side of the jacuzzi. I take in a toned bronzed torso with a tattoo snaking around the shoulder before it slips under the water.

It's the man I met in reception, Jake, and he's giving me a lopsided smile.

"Mind if I join you?"

Hell, I'm not going to turn that body away. And besides, he's already in the pool.

"Sure."

I half close my eyes again, trying to recapture the relaxing feeling, but I'm too aware of the hot man in the pool with me. Through half-closed eyes, I study him.

He's got his arms stretched out around the edge of the pool, and the tattoo continues over his shoulder and down one arm. It's a series of intricate patterns with a name entwined: Riley. Great. He's got a wife, although I note no wedding ring. Must be a girlfriend. Then why is he flirting with me? Because I'm absolutely sure that he is.

I snap my eyes fully closed, determined not to flirt with the hot, almost naked man in the pool with me who has his girlfriend's name tattooed on his arm.

"Have you been here before?"

I open one eye lazily and give him a look. I mean, come on. That's the pick-up equivalent of 'Do you come here often?'

He's looking at me expectantly, and damn, his face is as striking as his body. He has a shaggy beard and intense brown eyes with a flirty sparkle to them.

What can it hurt to have a conversation? I don't need to flirt.

"First time."

"Me too. I was supposed to meet a buddy, but his kid got sick."

He lifts his arm in the air in a shrug, and I notice a colorful bracelet on his arm. It's all pink beads and heart shapes strung together on an elastic band.

He sees me looking and holds up his arm so I can see the bracelet.

"My little girl made this for me."

Okay, so he's got a girlfriend and a kid. This guy's got some nerve getting into the pool with me all smiley and chatty.

"Her name's Riley." He smiles fondly as his hand runs over the bracelet.

Ahh, so it's the kid's name tattooed on him. That makes sense.

"How old is she?"

"She's almost three." His expression softens as he talks about his little girl. "She'll talk your ear off. Always bossing me around."

He looks up at me suddenly and gives a surprised chuckle. "This is my first night away from her since her mother left, and I'm already talking about her."

"That's understandable."

Noted also about the absent mother. Is this guy deliberately letting me know he's single? I decide I don't care. He's hot, and I've been ordered to relax. Why not have a little flirt?

I slide up a bit in the water so my arms and chest are on the surface. I catch his quick look to my breasts and the fleeting hungry expression that crosses his face.

A hot flush courses through my body knowing that he finds me desirable.

"Complimentary champagne?"

I turn at the sound of the waitress's voice.

"All our guests get a free glass of champagne to have in the jacuzzi."

She holds out a tray, and I take a glass of cold champagne. Jake does too.

"Cheers." He holds his glass up to me, and I slide forward to bump his glass. He slides forward at the same time, and our legs collide.

I feel a jolt run through me at his touch, and it sets me off balance. I slide off the ledge, and his arm shoots out to steady me. I'm giggling because I feel ridiculous sliding around the jacuzzi, but these damn seats are making me slip.

He's still holding me, and his grip is strong and steady.

"You okay?"

"Yeah. Seems I only need a sip of champagne to set me off."

He chuckles and lets me go as I regain my balance. Now I'm sitting closer to him, where his arm can easily touch me and our knees bump together in the water.

I'm aware of a new tension building in me, and this one has nothing to do with my sick mom. This is a tension that's concentrated in the core of my body, and there's only one way I know how to release it.

A few hours later and I pad out of the changing room, feeling lightheaded from the champagne. Jake is coming out of the men's changing area, and he turns to wait when he sees me.

"What floor you headed to?"

We spent the last two hours talking and flirting with our legs bumping under the water.

I've learned he's a single dad, and he's here to relax. I've told him all about my mom and why I'm here too.

We've talked about our families, our jobs, and we've laughed a lot. We agreed to meet downstairs for dinner. But now here he is, looking almost as good dressed in casual jeans and a checkered shirt, with his hair shaggy and wet, as he did half naked.

"Ninth floor."

His eyes light up. "Same."

We get in the elevator together, and I'm aware of how close he is. He turns to me and is about to say something when another guest steps into the elevator.

He shuts his mouth, and we ride in silence.

His fingers brush against my thigh, and my breath catches at his touch. I keep my gaze ahead and gently press my thigh against his fingers, letting him know I like his touch.

His hand moves slowly up my thigh while we both keep our gazes forward.

The elevator stops on the fourth floor, and the guest gets out.

As soon as the doors close, we turn to each other. Our lips collide and it's a passionate, urgent kiss. Our tongues tangle as his hands run over my body, causing my skin to heat.

He pushes me against the back of the elevator and presses himself into me, letting me feel his hardness.

My breath quickens. I've got a stranger pressed against me, and it feels fantastic.

"I want you, Fiona." He breathes the words into my

ear, making my whole body shiver and sending a wave of heat between my legs.

"I want you too, Jake."

Because right now I do. I don't know if it's the champagne, or being away, or the sheer magnetic pull of him, but I want this man. And I want him now.

"Come back to my room."

My body tenses. I know what that means. But with all the things that have been going on in my life lately, this feels good. This feels real and urgent, and it's what I need.

"Okay."

He looks at me with those intense eyes.

"Let's be clear. I want your body, Fiona. That's all." His hands run over my breasts and I tilt my head back as he palms them, his breathing coming short and sharp. "This is for this weekend only. I don't do relationships."

He's pressed against me with his package rubbing against my panties. His words should sting, but instead they make my body quiver.

A weekend of no strings sex. My body shivers in anticipation. "Fine with me."

The elevator dings, and we jump apart as the doors open.

He takes me by the hand, and I follow him down the corridor. I came here to relax, and that's exactly what I'm going to do.

3

JAKE

I pull Fiona into my hotel room and slide the key into the slot. The lights flicker on, illuminating the plain but functional hotel furnishings.

My dick's as hard as a rock and I want to get it in this curvy beauty, but first I want to see all of that delicious body.

I click the door shut and pull her toward the bed.

"Get undressed."

She gives me a raised eyebrow look at my commanding tone, but she must like it because she reaches for her blouse and starts undoing the top button. But she's moving too fast. I want a show, not a quick undressing.

I stop her hand. "Slow down."

I spin her around and sit on the bed so I'm facing her. "I want to watch."

"You want a show, do you?"

"Yes." That's exactly what I want. She licks her lips and

slowly unbuttons her blouse. Her eyes stay on mine, but I let mine rove over her.

She's a beauty all right, with big bouncy tits and wide, grabbable hips.

She undoes the last button, and she's wearing a white cotton bra.

"Take it off."

My dick's pushing against my jeans, and I shimmy out of them. She unhooks her bra and trails her hands over her tits, twirling her nipples.

Her nipples are dark circles, and as her fingers run over them, they pebble, hard.

I pull my dick out of my boxers and stroke along its length as I watch her play with herself. A bit of pre-cum shoots out of me, and I know I need to get this party moving or I'm going to shoot my load before I even get inside her.

"Come here."

I reach a hand out and take her hips. She's got a skirt on, and it's easy to slide it off and her panties as well.

Now she's completely naked, and I take a sharp intake of breath.

She sure is a beauty. With her hair hanging wet over her shoulders and a smile on her lips, a man could get used to having a woman like this around. Except I don't want any woman around.

I'll take what I need from her, and what I need is for her to be riding my cock.

She comes forward and straddles me on the bed, and I get the musky scent of her pussy. My heart's beating hard in my chest. It's been a long time since I had the opportunity to be with a woman, but I remember what to do.

She's hovering over my dick, but I put my hand out to pause her.

"I'll get a condom."

I reach for my wallet and pull it out. It's been sitting in there for a while, but the last thing I want is another kid to look after.

She helps me slide on the condom, then lines herself up over my cock.

I run my dick over her slit, making sure she's nice and wet. Her head tilts back, and her tits are right in my face. I grab a nipple in my mouth as I slowly ease myself into her. She moans, a delicious high-pitched noise that lets me know she's enjoying it.

I pull her down my shaft, going all the way in. She cries out at the shock, but she feels so damn good I don't want to ease up. I hold her hips and slide her up and down my cock, pumping myself into her as hard as I can.

Her tits jiggle in my face, and I lick at her nipple. She cries out and grabs me around the shoulders, thrusting herself down on me.

I can feel the tension building, and I'm not going to last long like this.

I'm taking what I want from this woman. I'm fucking her at the pace I want, burrowing my dick inside her tight pussy. And she loves it. She's moaning, and her cries are getting shorter and sharper.

I pull her down hard on my dick, and she cries out. Her pussy contracts so hard that it literally sucks everything out of me. I explode with the force of a train wreck, shooting cum so hard I feel a snap.

"Oh shit."

She catches my worried tone. "What is it?"

I'm scrambling to get her off me, and she looks confused. I pull the condom out by the neck, but I already know what I'm going to find.

I came so hard I broke the condom.

4

FIONA

Jake looks alarmed as he takes in the broken condom.

"Are you on the pill?"

I shake my head.

"Shit." He runs a hand through his hair, looking more terrified then he should. It's only a broken condom.

"I can get the morning after pill."

I slide off him and start pulling my clothes on. It's not ideal, but what can you do when something like this happens? I don't want to get pregnant from a one-night stand.

"Yeah, I think you'd better. Is there a pharmacy at the resort?"

I think about the website and try to remember what's on site. We're pretty remote, and I don't remember a pharmacy.

"I don't think so."

"Shit."

He's looking really worried now, and I run a hand reassuringly over his shoulder.

"You can take it up to seventy-two hours after, so I can stop by a pharmacy on my way home on Sunday."

He looks up at me questioningly.

"Not that I've ever taken it before," I add hastily. "In fact, I've never done this before." He raises his eyebrows, because I'm pretty sure my brazen performance just now shows I'm not a virgin. "Sex with a stranger, I mean."

Although I don't want to say it, but after knowing Jake for only a few hours, he doesn't feel like a stranger.

He grabs his phone and starts tapping. "I'm just going to check on that seventy-two hour thing."

I feel a pang of hurt that he doesn't trust me.

"My mother's a family planning nurse, or was before she got sick. She drummed it into us. I'm sure it's seventy-two hours."

He looks up from his phone, and his hand runs down my arm.

"I don't mean to doubt you. It's just that I've already got one child to care for. I don't want another."

I get where he's coming from, but I still feel a pang of disappointment. Which doesn't make sense. I've just met this guy. Of course he doesn't want a child with me, and I don't want one with him.

Only they would be cute, with his shaggy dark hair and big brown eyes.

I shake my head to clear it. What the hell am I thinking about children for at a time like this?

He finds what he's looking for on his phone.

"You're right. Seventy-two hours, although forty-eight hours is better."

I do the calculations in my head.

"I'm leaving Sunday afternoon; I'll stop at the first pharmacy I see."

"I'll come with you."

Wow. He really doesn't trust me. I turn away to pull my top on so he doesn't see the expression on my face.

"If you really must."

He must sense my hurt, because he stands up and takes my arm.

"It's not that I don't trust you, Fiona. It's just I know how easily pregnancy can happen."

"Is that what happened to you?"

He nods.

"Riley was a happy accident. I'd only been seeing her mother for a few months. I thought she was on the pill, but she was forgetful.

"I didn't know that at the time; there was a lot I didn't know about her. Like her little drug habit." His voice turns bitter.

"I thought I loved her. I thought we could give it a try when Riley came along, but it was too much responsibility for her. I woke up one morning, and she was gone. Left Riley and a note."

He turns away, running his fingers through his hair. "Sorry, you don't want to hear all this."

It's the first time since I met him that he's shown a vulnerable side. I'm not sure why he's opening up to me, but I'm happy to listen if that's what he needs.

I put my hand on his arm. "It's fine, really." I give him a

lopsided smile. "Why don't we raid the mini bar, and you can tell me as much or as little as you like?"

He grins and plants a kiss on my lips. This one is tender, not as rough and urgent as before.

"That sounds like a great idea."

"I'll race you to the boat."

Jake drops the bags in surprise as I take off down the jetty, the wooden slats thumping under my feet.

I'm almost at the boat when he grabs me around the waist.

"Oh no you don't."

I'm laughing as he tries to lift me out of the way, but I kick out my foot and it touches the stern. I let out a triumphant shout.

"I won!"

"Oh yeah?"

He tickles me until I fall to the floor laughing, and he springs aboard with a triumphant look on his face.

"I'm the first one on the boat. I won."

"You cheated."

He reaches out a hand to help me up.

"Don't be a sore loser." But his eyes are sparkling with laughter.

It's the following day, and Jake invited me out on a fishing trip with him. I used to fish with my dad so I happily accepted. Besides, I'm hoping to get a little more of what we did last night.

We stayed up chatting most of the night and made love again twice. Since I'm getting the morning after pill anyway, we dispensed with protection, and the raw sensation of his dick inside me was the best feeling.

As the sky started turning pink, I snuck back to my room for a couple of hours sleep, but not before promising to meet him for fishing today.

As we push off from the jetty, I lean back. The gentle spray from the lake hits my face, and the sun instantly warms it. I close my eyes, enjoying the sensation, my face turned up to the sun.

I realize that for the first time since Mom got sick, I feel truly relaxed.

I told Jake all about Mom last night, the care and treatment. And he told me all about his ex and his heartbreak. How it changed him, made him harder.

That may be the case, but I'm seeing glimpses of his soft side. He's fun to be with and easygoing. I guess that's what happens when you know there are no strings attached.

There's a fishing spot he's been told about on the other side of one of the small islands. It doesn't take long to get there, and he anchors the boat and gets the lines ready.

I can tell he's impressed that I know how to bait a line, but when you grow up in a small town with a rugged dad, this is what you do for fun.

"Do you want to make things interesting?" I ask as I hook the bait onto my line.

"What do you mean?" He eyes me suspiciously.

"Put a little wager on who catches the biggest fish."

He raises his eyebrows. "You think you can out fish me?"

"I know I can." It's confident talk. I haven't fished in

years, but I'm enjoying the banter between us and the way his eyes sparkle.

"Those are fighting words, missy."

"Ten dollars in, winner takes all."

It's a small wager, but it'll keep things interesting.

He holds out his hand. "Done." I take his hand to shake on the deal, and he holds onto my hand tightly, forcing me to look up at him. "And loser buys the dinner."

I meet his eyes, and my heartbeat goes up a notch. He wants to have dinner with me.

The thought makes my heart flutter, although I'm sure it's only because having dinner is bound to lead to having more sex.

I'm supposed to have a massage booked later, but hey, I'm here to relax, and being wined and dined by a man that makes me laugh and then having hot sex all night is still relaxing.

I pump his hand.

"You're on."

5

JAKE

The sound of birdsong wakes me, and I stretch lazily. My body feels heavy and relaxed, and I snuggle back under the covers.

It was another amazing night with Fiona. She made me laugh so hard over dinner, which I didn't mind paying for since she caught the biggest fish.

The resort has a huge fireplace, and we stayed up chatting by the fire until the staff gave us a polite hurry along.

Then there was the sex. I smile just thinking about it. We turned the shower on and made love slowly, soaping each other up and exploring each other's bodies.

I licked her until she came and then fucked her against the shelf in the shower so hard that I broke the soap dispenser right off the wall.

I laugh at the memory. And realize my sides hurt. I've done a lot of laughing over the last few days.

I reach out to the other side of the bed, but it's cold. Fiona insisted on going back to her room to sleep, since this is only a causal thing. But the truth is, I missed her body pressed against mine.

I wonder if she's up yet. We agreed to meet today for a hike that she wants to do to some hot springs in the mountain.

It'll be the last time I see her before our weekend fling is over. I feel a pang in my chest at the thought. This was supposed to be a causal thing, but the more time I spend with her, the more I want to see her again.

I roll out of bed and check my phone. It's nine-thirty. I must have slept in. We agreed to meet at nine.

We haven't exchanged phone numbers, and she was going to knock at my door to get me. I wonder if she knocked and I didn't answer. But you become a light sleeper when you're a parent. I'm sure I would have heard.

And I didn't drink anything last night. I wanted to hang with her while sober, to see if she still made me laugh, and to see if the sex was still good. She did, and it was.

When I first saw Fiona, I thought this would be a fling. But we've had such a good time, I know I have to see her again. A woman that hot who knows how to fish. I can't walk away from that.

She lives in Bosun River, which is a two hours' drive from Maple Springs. But there's a connection between us. I can make that distance work. Before we leave today, I'm going to get her number and make a plan to see her again.

I get out of bed feeling good and have a stretch. My body feels heavy and lethargic from all the sex and so super relaxed.

Fiona probably feels the same and must have overslept

like I did. It was almost 4.a.m. when she crept back to her room.

I'm pulling my sweatpants on when a piece of paper by the door catches my eye. It's folded in half and looks like it's been pushed under the door.

I unfold the paper, and there's a scribbled note written on the hotel stationary.

My mom's taken a turn for the worse and I have to leave.
Thanks for an amazing weekend.
Fiona xx

I read the note twice, with a tight feeling in my chest. She's gone.

I turn the note over in my hand, but there's nothing on the back. No phone number. I don't even know her last name.

She still thinks this was a fling to me. And now I can't tell her that it was more, much more.

I grab the phone next to the bed and call reception. It might not be too late.

"The guest in room 909, has she checked out?"

"She checked out at six a.m. this morning."

My heart sinks. She's really gone. My mind whirls, wondering how I can get her information.

"I've got some things of hers and don't know where to return them. Can you give me her address, please?"

There's a pause. "I'm sorry, sir. We can't give out guest information."

"But we're friends. We know each other."

"I'm sorry, sir. It's hotel policy. If you call your friend, I'm sure she can give you her address."

I bite my lip.

"The thing is I've lost her number. Can you remind me of it again?"

There's a polite pause. "I'm sorry. We can't give out that information."

"Can you at least give me her last name?"

"I'm sorry, sir. We don't give out guest information." The voice is curt, and I don't blame them. She's a female on her own. They can't give out her info to any random guy who calls.

I hang up the phone in frustration and sink into the bed. She's gone.

She's left, and I don't even know her full name. All I've got is the town she lives in.

It's my own fault. I was so quick to tell her that I only wanted a fling and too slow to tell her my feelings had changed.

I thought I could go around being Mister Tough Guy and harden my heart to the world. But the only person I've hurt is myself.

6

FIONA

Six months later…

"**O**hh, look at this one."

Karen holds up a tiny, knitted cardigan in pale yellow. The sleeves are so tiny I can barely imagine a baby in them.

I take if off her and turn the soft fabric over in my hands. It's hand knitted, and some of the thread is starting to unravel at the seams. But it's not in bad shape for a secondhand cardigan.

If Mom was still here, she'd be able to fix that up easily. There's a pain in my chest so sudden and sharp that I squeeze my eyes shut.

"Are you okay?"

Karen's voice sounds alarmed, and I take a deep breath and open my eyes. She's looking at me with concern.

"Yeah fine. Just thinking about Mom."

Karen rubs my shoulder gently. "You want to go home?"

"No." I put my shoulders back resolutely. It's been over five months since Mom passed, and while the grief is still there, each time it gets a little less.

Her illness was a long one, and I know her passing brought her a sense of peace. But it doesn't stop me from missing her and especially with the baby on its way.

I rub my round belly, and as always, a sense of calm comes over me. I already know it's a girl, and I'll name her after my mom.

I found out I was pregnant the day after Mom's funeral. With death comes renewal and new life, and the baby growing inside of me is my reminder of that.

"He was asking around for you again yesterday."

Karen looks at me in a pointed way, and I try not to let her see the way my heart leaps at her words.

I tuck the cardigan under my arm and keep searching the racks.

"He came into the diner again. Was really quizzing Barney about you."

I finish with the rack and turn to the next one. My heart's racing, but I keep my voice causal.

"What did Barney say?"

"He said what I told him to say. That he didn't know a Fiona or anyone with your description and that he must have the wrong town."

I feel relief but also sadness.

"Thanks Karen."

"He doesn't like it, you know. Said the poor guy looked tired and ragged and lovesick. He said if he comes again, he's going to tell him the truth."

I spin around. "No Karen, he can't."

She puts her hands on her hips. "Why not, Fiona? The guy's obviously obsessed with you if he's still looking for you after what, six months? Why not just speak to him at least, put him out of his misery?"

What she says makes sense, but I can't let him see me like this, six months pregnant.

"You know why."

She glances down at my round belly.

"He has a right to know."

"He won't want to know, believe me. The guy's already raising one kid solo. He made it quite clear he doesn't want another."

"All men say that. Look at Barney. He swore he didn't want a big family, but he loves having them all running around and jumping on him."

Her eyes go soft as she talks about her husband. "Men don't always know what they want, and we have to show them."

"It's not just that. I swore I'd take the morning after pill, take care of it, and I broke that promise. I forgot."

"Fiona, your mom was dying. You can be forgiven."

For a moment, I'm transported back to that morning. My body relaxed and drowsy and the phone call from my brother telling me that Mom had taken an unexpected turn. I packed and left immediately.

For the next two weeks, I didn't leave Mom's side. We all knew it was her final days, and all we could do was make her as comfortable as possible and be there for her.

In the quiet times, I yearned for Jake. I imagined talking to him about what I was going through. I imagined leaning into him, with his strong arms around me for comfort.

It was silly, I know. He made it clear he was only after some fun, but the thought of his arms around me is what got me through those dark weeks and the ones that followed.

When I found out the baby was on the way, it was a shock, but I knew immediately I wanted to keep her. Coming so close after Mom's death, it had to be a sign.

"He doesn't want a relationship with me, Karen. He made it clear, remember? It was a weekend fling. He told me that's all it was. I'm perfectly capable of raising this baby on my own."

She raises her eyebrows. "Is that why we're buying baby clothes from a charity shop?"

I rub my temples, because she's right. Money will be tough.

"We'll manage." Because we have to. "He was clear. It was a fling, and that's it."

"Oh yeah? Then why is he searching the town for you?"

I turn my attention back to the racks of clothes. Because she's right. I have no idea why he's still looking for me six months after our fling.

7

JAKE

My eyes scan the crisscrossing pathways like they always do while one arm pushes lazily at the swing.

"Daddy, it's too high."

I snap my attention to Riley, her legs sticking out of the swing at a jaunty angle. I grab the swing and slow it down until it comes to stop.

"What do you want to play on next?"

I lift her out of the swing, and she fixes me with a huffy look.

"I want to go home."

Ignoring her request, I glance around the park to see if there's a free bench.

"Should we have our picnic on the blue bench or the yellow bench today?"

She folds her arms and sticks her bottom lip out. "No lunch here. I want to go home."

"Come on, sweetie. We can have lunch and then go on the slide for a bit."

"I don't like this park, Daddy."

It's midday on a Saturday, and the park is teeming with other children.

I chose this one because it's in the center of Bosun River and paths crisscross around it.

I'm hoping Fiona might walk down one of these paths. I've been hoping for the last six months, bringing Riley here every weekend that I can. It's a long drive from Maple Springs, and at first, she saw it as an adventure, but lately it's been an effort to get her into the car.

"I want to go to the park near daycare. Where Avery goes."

She's referring to a daycare friend. And the park she means is always teeming with Maple Springs kids that she knows. She doesn't understand why I drag her out here.

It's been six months, and no matter where I look and who I ask, there's no sign of Fiona. It's like she doesn't want to be found.

I look at my daughter, her lip sticking out. She's right. She should be playing with her friends, not traipsing halfway across the state so I can chase down a one-night stand who might not even be interested. Maybe it's time to give up.

I crouch down so I'm eye level with Riley.

"Okay, pumpkin. We'll play here today, and next weekend, we'll play at the daycare park."

She smiles cautiously. "I don't want to come back to this one, Daddy."

I nod. I've got to put my daughter first and move on. My chest tightens at the thought, but I don't know what else I can do.

"Okay, pumpkin. After today, we won't come back."

She beams and throws her tiny arms around my neck in a ferocious hug. "I love you, Daddy."

"I love you too, sweetie."

She skips off to the slide and I stand up slowly, watching her go.

I've tried everything to look for Fiona, if that was even her name. She gave me the best weekend I'd had in years, but maybe that's all it was meant to be.

It's time to let her go.

That's when I see the figure emerging from the trees that line the play area. She's walking away from the playground. I mustn't have noticed her when I was talking with Riley. But I notice her now. I'd recognize that ass anywhere, and the long dark hair hanging down her back.

My heart leaps in my chest. After six months of searching, it's her. Fiona.

I glance over to Riley, and she's playing happily on the slide fort with another girl.

The playground has a low colorful fence running around it. It's a big enclosure, and I jog to the other end where Fiona's path runs alongside.

"Fiona!"

The figure keeps walking, and I pick up my speed. I'm at the end of the playground area when I call out again.

This time she turns. Her face registers surprise when she sees me. There's a flash of happiness, and then it's replaced by something neutral.

"Hey," I call out, catching my breath.

She half turns and she's as beautiful as I remember, flashing green eyes and full lips. I can't speak for a moment. All the prepared lines from the last six months desert me.

"I was playing at the park with Riley. I thought that was you."

I try to sound casual, like I haven't been hunting her down for the last six months.

She nods, but she doesn't look surprised to see me, and I wonder if she knows I've been asking around for her.

"Yup, it's me."

She's only half turned on the path, as if she can't wait to get moving again and I'm holding her up. I have a sinking sensation. She's not as happy to see me as I am to see her.

"You left in such a hurry. How is your mom?"

Her face falls, and I realize my mistake.

"She passed away."

"I'm so sorry."

Her shoulders hunch, and I feel like as ass. I've dreamed about this moment, and two seconds in I'm making her cry.

I shimmy over the playground fence and join her on the path, my arm going around her shoulders instinctually.

"Hey, I'm sorry for your loss."

She shakes her head and wipes her eyes.

"It's fine. I'm okay, really. Just a bit emotional these days."

She turns fully, and my hand falls off her shoulder as I get a look at her properly. Her belly is sticking out in a round bump that can only mean one thing. My chest constricts.

"You're pregnant."

I can't breathe for a moment. In all the scenarios I ran over in my head, I didn't expect this. She must have a boyfriend, but the bump looks like she's quite far along.

"How far?"

"Six months."

It's been about six months since we met. Did she have a boyfriend then?

She's watching me carefully. And finally, I get it.

"It's mine?"

My mind's racing. She's pregnant with my baby. I take a step back, trying to process it.

"You didn't take the pill?"

She shakes her head. "Mom was sick. I went back immediately, and it slipped my mind. I spent the next two week caring for her."

She must have gone through so much, and I should have been there for her.

"Why didn't you tell me?"

I mean about her mom, but she must think I'm talking about the baby, because she recoils.

"You made it clear you weren't interested, that you didn't want another baby."

I think back to that weekend and know she's right. I was putting on this hard persona, too busy telling her what I didn't want that I never told her what I did want. That I wanted her.

"How could I have told you anyway? I didn't have your number. There was no way, even if I wanted to."

The words hurt.

"And you didn't want to?"

She looks down.

"I had a great time with you Jake."

This doesn't sound good. My voice sounds desperate when I speak. "I did too. I had the best time."

"But can you honestly tell me that this is what you want?"

She indicates her round belly, the baby growing inside her.

It's too much to process. I knew her for a weekend. I was so sure about us. But I didn't expect this.

"Daddy, Daddy."

My attention is pulled back to the playground and Riley running toward me from the other side of the fence.

When I look back to Fiona, she's smiling sadly. "I'm going now, Jake."

"Daddy, I want to go home."

Riley has a huffy look on her face, and there's a mark on her knee like she's fallen over.

I turn back to Fiona, and I know this is when I'm meant to say something, tell her how much I've missed her, but I'm frozen. It's all too much to take in, and my daughter needs me.

"Goodbye Jake." Fiona turns and walks away, and I watch her go. The perfect woman with a less than perfect scenario.

"Can we go now, Daddy?"

"Yes, pumpkin." I pull my attention back to my daughter. "We can go."

8

FIONA

I scoop the ice cream out of the tub and straight into my mouth. I close my eyes, savoring the chocolate flavor. If there's one good thing about pregnancy, it gives you an excuse to eat. Today my craving is chocolate ice cream, and this is my third spoonful.

I take one more and put the lid back on.

Just then the doorbell rings, and I hastily shove the tub back into the freezer.

"Just a minute." I give the spoon a quick lick and drop it in the sink before heading to the entranceway.

I open the door, and Jake is standing there.

My heart skips a beat. His hair is messy, and his beard is in need of a trim. The ruggedness only highlights his natural good looks.

"Can I come in?"

I hesitate. I've spent the week going over our encounter in the park, and it comes back to the same thing. I was right all along. He was only after a fling, and he tracked me down hoping he could continue that. He didn't say anything in the park to make me think otherwise.

It's too late for flings now. I have to do what's best for me and the baby.

"How did you find me?" I guess Karen or Barney must have caved and given out my address.

"I followed you from the park."

Okay, that's a bit creepy.

"I know it sounds creepy." It's like he read my mind. "But I knew I wouldn't get another opportunity; I've been looking for you everywhere. But I couldn't speak to you with Riley around."

I don't know whether to be freaked out that he followed me or impressed.

"I'm not sure, Jake."

His hands go up in the air in a conciliatory gesture. "I want to explain."

I guess I owe him that. He's looking so sincere that I decide to give him the benefit of the doubt. And besides, there's a part of me that still longs for him, that still hopes he wants to be with me.

"Come in." I open the door, and he follows me into the kitchen. "You want coffee?"

While I make the coffee, he leans on the kitchen counter, watching me.

"I don't run away from my responsibilities, Fiona. If the baby's mine, I want to be involved."

So, he's come for the baby and not me. I stir the coffee slowly, trying to hide my disappointment. But of course he's come for the baby. Did I really expect otherwise?

"I'm a good father. I mean, sometimes Riley has on

odd socks, and I never iron her clothes. The house is a mess, and she hasn't had a haircut for a year. But I love her more than anything in the world. I love spending time with her. We play dragons and princesses together, and I mostly play the princess. I cut the crusts off her sandwiches, I read to her every night, mostly the same book over and over, and sometimes she climbs into the bed with me and we sleep snuggled up together."

I smile despite myself, picturing him as the messy but loving father. I think about how nice that would be for my little girl.

"It will be good for Riley to have a sibling; someone she can play with. I've got dad experience now; I can look after this kid."

He puts his coffee down, and his tone becomes earnest.

"I'm a good dad, Fiona. Sure, it's damned hard work, but I'll do it again. I want to do it again. I have a steady job, and I can provide for you and the baby."

I take a sip of my decaf coffee, playing for time. I hear what he's saying. He's perfect father material. But if that's all he wants, to swoop in here and be the hero dad, then I'm not interested.

"We'll be fine on our own, Jake. I've got my brother and my friends to help. I can look after the baby on my own."

His face falls, and maybe I'm being too harsh.

"I mean, if you want to be involved, we can do weekend visits or something. That would be okay. But don't worry about us. We'll be fine on our own."

He puts his coffee down. "I don't think you understand."

His hands go to my shoulders, and the warmth in them is so familiar, what I've yearned for all these weeks. The feeling is so powerful it almost throws me off balance.

"It's not the baby I'm here for. It's you." My breath catches in my throat. "That weekend we spent together, it was special. I've never felt like that before, about anyone."

I scan his face, looking for any hidden meaning, but his eyes are wide and he looks genuine.

"It was never like this with Riley's mom. We got along, but I never felt like this. I know it was only two days, Fiona. But I love you. I want to be with you, and if that means having another baby, then that's what we'll do."

I can't breathe. It's everything I've wanted him to say, everything I imagined over the last six months.

"But the baby? I was meant to get the pill, and I let you down."

"Oh sweetie, you didn't let me down. I wish I could have been there for you over that dark time. But you didn't let me down. You've given me a gift. I learned that with Riley. It was so hard looking after a baby at first, and I thought we'd made a big mistake. But when I surrendered to parenthood, I realized what a gift it is. I want to do that with you."

His arms go around me, and I lean into his chest. He feels solid and stable and safe.

"I've thought about you so much over the last six months." It all comes out; I tell him how it was the thought of him that got me through the darkest times.

He kisses the top of my head. "I'm here for you now. Forever."

My heart warms at his words. "Me too."

"I've spent the last six months trying to track you down. It seems no one in this town knows you at all."

I look up at him, feeling sheepish.

"I might have told them not to tell you anything. I thought you wouldn't want to know, after what you said when we met."

"Oh sweetie, I was so stupid. I thought I was done with women, but you showed me I could have fun again, be free and happy. I love you so much."

"I love you too."

He squeezes me tight, and I feel the baby kick. I know with Jake by my side, we'll be fine. And I know Mom is looking down on us and smiling.

EPILOGUE

FIONA

Five years later…

There's a squeal from the garden, and I peer out of the upstairs window.

Riley is on the trampoline holding her sister Jenny's hands. As they jump up, they tuck their legs up, squealing, playing a game only they know the rules to.

"What are they doing?" I mutter.

Rough hands slide around my waist, and I lean into Jake as he nuzzles up behind me.

"They're playing, and they're fine."

He's right. They're on the trampoline in our gated back yard. If they're happy playing together, it's always best to leave them.

"The baby's asleep."

He says it against my neck as he nips at my skin. A delicious shiver runs through me.

Tom isn't quite a baby anymore at two years old, but he still likes an afternoon nap.

"I figure we've got about five minutes before one of them hurts themselves or wants a snack, so…"

He's already pulling at my skirt, lifting the fabric over my thighs.

"What do you have in mind?"

I press myself against him and feel his hard-on pressing back.

"I think you know what I have in mind."

I giggle as his hand slides up my thigh. I never knew parenting would be full of so many quickies.

He slides my panties down, and I turn around to undo his belt. As I pull his dick out of his pants, he pushes me back onto the bed.

My skirt falls open, and his eyes go dark as he gazes between my legs. I open my legs wide, letting him have a full view, knowing how much it turns him on.

"Damn, girl. I need that pussy."

He grabs his cock, and with one hand on my thigh, lines it up with my entrance.

I'm already wet for him and he slides straight into me, making me gasp. His cock feels familiar now, and he knows just what to do with it. I wrap my legs around him and push my hips upward, pulling him deeper into me.

He groans, and I know I've hit his sweet spot like he's hit mine.

As he moves above me my clit rubs against him, and in a few minutes, I know I can't hold on anymore.

I stifle my cries as I come, and he releases at the same time I do. We push together, squeezing hold of each other through the orgasm.

Afterward, he kisses me gently.

"That was the preview. I'll give you the full show tonight."

I know he will. The older kids are staying at their cousins' tonight. And once Tom is in bed, we'll get in the jacuzzi we had installed in the bathroom, pour the champagne, and make love slowly.

There's a shout from outside, and I look out to see Riley storming off in a huff.

It was a nice interlude, but it looks like we're back on parenting duty. And I couldn't be happier.

WHAT TO READ NEXT

Four brothers, four steamy love stories.
Will Jake's brothers find their happily ever afters?
Zoey - Nick & Zoey
Jake - Jake & Fiona
The SEAL's Obsession - Trent & Lina
Fudge & the Firefighter - Davis & Serena

Fudge & The Firefighter

Serena

My neighbor, the firefighter, the man so hot my panties melt every time I pass him on the stairs. Because yeah, I've started taking the stairs just so I can 'accidentally' run into him; that's how bad I've got the hots for this guy.

When I accidentally burn my Christmas fudge and set off the smoke alarm, I don't expect him to break down my door on a one-man rescue mission.

But once I'm in his arms, there's no turning back. It's

Christmas Eve, I'm feeling bold, and this is one Christmas gift I'm going to enjoy unwrapping.

Davis

I've watched the curvy goddess across the hall for the past few months. The delicious baking smells coming from her apartment make my mouth water almost as much as her curves.

When she's in danger, I leap at the chance to be her hero.

But once I've got her in my arms, I'm the one who needs rescuing. She's got me heart, body, and soul.

This is one tasty Christmas treat I want to enjoy all year round.

Fudge & the Firefighter is a forced-proximity, steamy instalove romance, featuring a smoking hot firefighter and the curvy girl he claims for Christmas.

Keep reading for an exclusive excerpt.

FUDGE & THE FIREFIGHTER

CHAPTER ONE

Serena

There's the clinking of glass on the other end of the phone and the sound of my mother taking a large slug of what I suspect is vodka.

"Ronaldo makes the best cocktails." My mom's voice is raspy, like she's been talking too much and smoking too many cigarettes.

"I'm sorry, honey. I'm several drinks in. They have their big celebrations on Christmas Eve in Portugal, you know."

I rub my temples, feeling the onset of a headache.

"Yes, you did mention that, Mother."

Like fifty times, I think, but I don't say. I'm happy my mom's found love again and is living it up in Portugal. I just wish she was more sober when she called.

She giggles, which is a sound I'm not sure a sixty something year old woman should make.

"We've had the loveliest time at his daughter's house. His children have been so welcoming."

"That's nice, Mom. I'm happy for you."

"They can't wait to meet you, honey. I told them how sorry we all were that you couldn't make it this year."

The truth is I have some money saved up and I could have gone with Mom, but the thought of intruding on someone else's Christmas makes me anxious. I don't want to be the spare wheel, hanging around and ruining their family traditions.

"Maybe next year," I say vaguely.

"I don't like the thought of you spending Christmas on your own, dear."

"I'm not spending Christmas on my own." It's a lie, but I can't stand my own mother feeling sorry for me.

"I don't suppose your dad bothered to invite you for Christmas?"

I can hear the stiffness in her voice.

"He sent me a card."

She snorts. "I suppose he's spending it with his latest girlfriend. What is she this time, a stripper?"

The disdain in Mom's voice makes me tense. She's the one that ended their marriage ten years ago, but she's never forgiven Dad for moving to Vegas and starting a new life.

"Not all women who live in Vegas are strippers, Mom."

"No, just the ones your father dates."

My head is pounding by now, and this is why I didn't want to spend Christmas with Mom. Because every time she has a few drinks at Christmas, she gets to bitching about Dad.

"What did Ronaldo get you?" I try changing the subject and reminding Mom about her new husband.

"Oh, a beautiful, diamanté-encrusted string bikini."

I shut my eyes and wonder if she's joking.

"I know, I know, but they appreciate older women here in Europe. They all wear bikinis well into their seventies."

She lowers her voice, and I can imagine her leaning in conspiratorially. "They even go topless, you know?"

"Please don't tell me you've been sunbathing topless, Mom."

She giggles. "When in Rome, or should I say when in Porto…" The giggle turns into a hearty chuckle that sounds laced with vodka.

"I've got to go, honey. It's time for me to give Ronaldo his Christmas present, if you know what I mean."

I can almost hear her winking down the phone.

"Oh Mom, no. You didn't need to tell me that."

Her tone goes mock innocent. "What honey, you think us old folks don't know how to have a little fun?"

Her voice drops to a whisper. "For an older man he's got so much vigor. He can go for hours."

"It's called Viagra, Mom."

"Oh no honey, it's the Mediterranean diet and all this sea air. I've never felt so frisky."

"Okay, Mom." I cut her off before she can say anything else that makes me feel nauseous. "I've got to go."

"I wish you'd find someone, Serena. You don't want to spend all your Christmases alone, dear."

I roll my eyes, and then remember she can't see me. Any conversation with Mom always comes back to my single status at some point.

"I've got to go, Mom."

"Merry Christmas, honey. I hope you have a nice day tomorrow with your friends."

"Merry Christmas, Mom."

I hang up the phone and sit on the bed staring at the blank screen.

I lied when I told Mom I was spending Christmas with friends. I'll be spending Christmas alone, cooking dinner for one and pigging out on my favorite homemade…

Beep Beep Beep.

"Fudge!"

The high-pitched wail of a smoke alarm pierces my eardrums.

I throw open the door to find smoke billowing from the kitchen. I must have forgotten to turn the burner off.

I race down the hall, almost going deaf as the wails from the smoke alarm assault my ears. Sure enough, there's a pot sitting on the stove with smoke streaming out of it.

"Shit."

I grab the pot off the stove and turn the burner off. Flames lick up the side of the pot, and I throw it in the sink and turn the tap on full blast.

Steam hisses as the flames go out, throwing a new cloud of smoke into the air and making me double over coughing.

Bang.

A loud noise makes me jump.

My eyes sting as I squint through the smoke. My front door is hanging open, and a large male figure emerges from the smokey haze.

He's carrying a fire extinguisher, but that's not what makes my jaw drop.

The only thing he's wearing is a towel wrapped around his waist. His body is ripped, a defined six pack with a curly trail of dark hair that leads enticingly under the towel.

The smoke clears, bringing his face into focus. Oh my god, it's the hot firefighter from across the hall. The guy I've been lusting over since I moved into this apartment three months ago.

"Where's the fire?"

I gulp as I take in his toned torso.

He'd better hose me down, because the only thing on fire here are my panties.

To keep reading visit:
mybook.to/FudgeFirefighter

GET YOUR FREE BOOK

Sign up to the Sadie King mailing list for a FREE book!

You'll be the first to hear about exclusive offers, bonus content and all the news from Sadie King.

To claim your free book visit:
www.authorsadieking.com/free

ABOUT THE AUTHOR

Sadie King is a USA Today Best Selling Author of short instalove romance.

She lives in New Zealand with her ex-military husband and raucous young son.

When she's not writing she loves catching waves with her son, running along the beach, and good wine, preferably drunk with a book in hand.

Keep in touch when you sign up for her newsletter. You'll even snag yourself a free short romance!

www.authorsadieking.com/free

www.ingramcontent.com/pod-product-compliance
Lightning Source LLC
Chambersburg PA
CBHW061403160726
47995CB00001B/445